MINNESOTA

WISCONSIN

S. DAKOTA

Decorah

Effigy Mounds

Marquette

Dubuque

Cedar River

Mason City

Clear Lake

Cedar Falls   Waterloo   Dyersville

Mississippi River

Lake Okoboji

Spirit Lake

Des Moines River

Orange City

Le Mars

Alta

Sioux City

Kate Shelley Bridge

Reiman Gardens

Boone

Ames

Amana Homestead

Cedar Rapids

Davenport

Iowa State Fair

Iowa River

Iowa City

Missouri River

Des Moines

Loess Hills

Covered Bridges of Madison County

St. Charles

Indianola

Knoxville

Ottumwa

Burlington

Council Bluffs

Sidney

NEBRASKA

MISSOURI

ILLINOIS

KANSAS

The Twelve Days of Christmas in Iowa

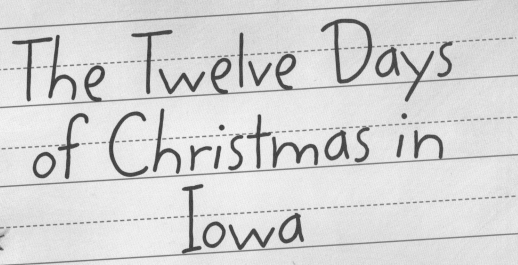

written and illustrated by
Sue F. Cornelison

STERLING

New York / London

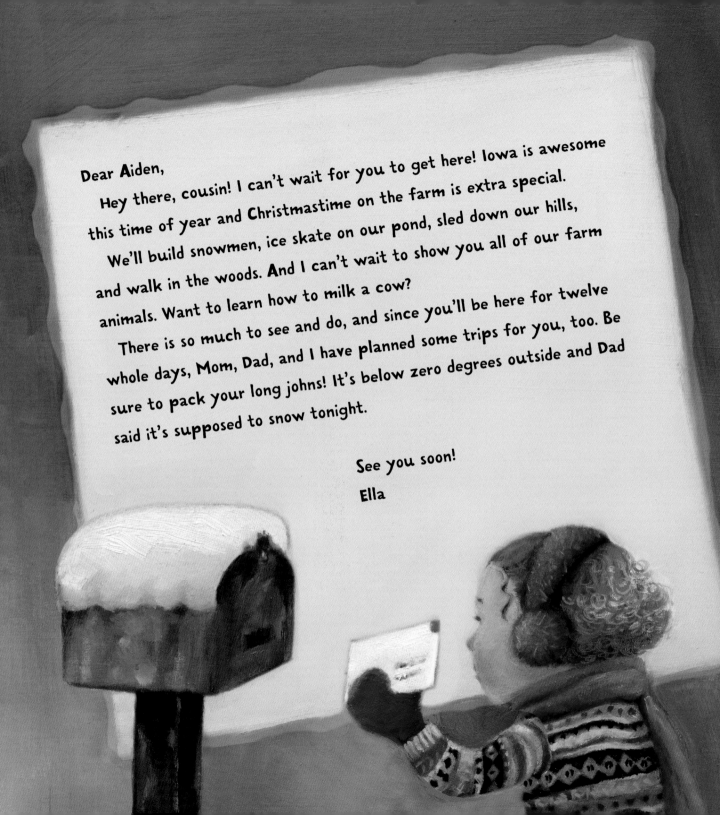

Dear Aiden,

Hey there, cousin! I can't wait for you to get here! Iowa is awesome this time of year and Christmastime on the farm is extra special.

We'll build snowmen, ice skate on our pond, sled down our hills, and walk in the woods. And I can't wait to show you all of our farm animals. Want to learn how to milk a cow?

There is so much to see and do, and since you'll be here for twelve whole days, Mom, Dad, and I have planned some trips for you, too. Be sure to pack your long johns! It's below zero degrees outside and Dad said it's supposed to snow tonight.

See you soon!
Ella

Dear Mom and Dad,

Brrrrrrrrrrrrrr. It's coooold here in Iowa. But we just put some logs on the fire and we're curled up in warm blankets, drinking hot chocolate. My toes have finally thawed and I'm warm and toasty now.

I sure wasn't warm this morning, though. Ella woke me up early. She was so excited to show me the newly fallen snow. The view out her window looked like a Christmas card! We couldn't get outside fast enough. We put on so many layers of clothes, I could hardly move. On our long walk through the woods, we spotted a goldfinch in an oak tree. That's a pretty cool combo: the official state bird and the official state tree! We also saw a young deer with his mom, a couple of wild turkeys, and even a giant bald eagle.

After our long walk back, I made my first snowman, and guess who landed right on his head? Yep, that little goldfinch! I could barely feel my toes, but boy, was that walk worth it!

I'll take a picture tomorrow of all this snow. You'll never believe it!

Aiden

On the first day of Christmas, my cousin gave to me . . .

a goldfinch in an oak tree.

Dear Mom and Dad,

Ella and I went out to the barn this morning to do chores. Can you believe that Aunt Sue and Uncle Ross have horses, cows, llamas, sheep, hens, AND two giant hogs?! Wilma and Wilbur are as big as bathtubs! And guess what? Wilma's going to have babies! They are due in two months! Ella's 4-H project is to feed and exercise her piglets until they are big enough to enter the Iowa State Fair in Des Moines in August. If they look anything like their parents, the piglets are sure to be blue-ribbon winners.

Ella says Iowa has the best state fair in the whole wide world. There is even a movie and a Broadway show based on it! Ella camps at the fair for ten straight days so she can show her hogs, then auctions them in the swine barn. She also competes in crazy contests like the cow chip toss and the turkey call. There are all kinds of rides and exhibits—including a life-size cow carved from butter! Most of the snacks at the fair are served on sticks, so you can walk and eat at the same time: pickles, pork chops, pineapples, and even salad on a stick . . . but Ella says the corn dog is the best. I want to try one! May I go next August? Please?

With love from your son who almost never begs, unless it's really, really important,

Aiden

On the second day of Christmas,
my cousin gave to me . . .

2 hefty hogs

and a goldfinch in an oak tree.

Hi, Mom and Dad,

Boy, do I have a story to tell you! Today we rode on an old train across the highest and longest double-track bridge in the world, the Kate Shelley Bridge in Boone (185 feet high and 2,685 feet long!). I was feeling pretty nervous. We were so high up that we could see for miles, and I could feel the bridge swaying in the wind! Then the conductor told us this incredible story: One night in 1881, a flood washed out the support timbers holding up one side of this bridge. A train carrying four men plunged into the river. A young girl named Kate Shelley heard the crash and decided she had to warn the conductor of the next train, which she knew would be crossing the bridge an hour later.

When her lantern went out, she dropped to her knees and crawled across the high bridge with only flashes of lightning to guide her. Once across the river, she ran another half mile to the train station to sound the alarm. The next train was carrying hundreds of passengers, but was stopped just in time, thanks to Kate. I felt a little silly for being such a chicken after hearing that story of bravery and heroism! She definitely deserves to have that bridge named after her!

See you soon,
Aiden

On the third day of Christmas,
my cousin gave to me . . .

3 train cars

2 hefty hogs,
and a goldfinch in an oak tree.

Dear Mom and Dad,

My new favorite way to travel is by hot air balloon! It was so peaceful and quiet floating high above the cornfields laced with snow. It took my breath away. No, not because it was so cold, but because it was so amazing! It was actually warm in the basket (the pros call it a "gondola") because of the hot air blowing up into the balloon.

Afterward, Uncle Ross took us to the Indianola National Balloon Museum, which was built to look like two upside-down balloons. Indianola and Warren County have hosted a hot air balloon festival for more than 40 years! The National Balloon Classic takes place every summer and balloonists from all over the world come to compete for prizes. Every competitor gets a map with targets marked and a whole bunch of little flour sacks. The players earn points by dropping the sacks closest to the targets. Doesn't that sound like the best game _ever_?

The museum had lots of awesome photos, too. My favorite was one called "The Night Glow." The balloons all lift off at once, glowing in the dark night sky like big glowing jack-o'-lanterns.

Way cool!
Aiden

On the fourth day of Christmas,
my cousin gave to me . . .

4 big balloons

3 train cars, 2 hefty hogs,
and a goldfinch in an oak tree.

Hi, Mom and Dad,

It may be cold outside, but inside it felt like summer in the Butterfly Wing of Reiman Gardens in Ames. There were butterflies of every shape, color, and size from all over the world, flying around in a big glass house! It's a really neat place to be, but if you two come here, you'll have to follow these rules: 1.) Don't grab the butterflies. They're very fragile and their wings are easily damaged. 2.) Watch where you step. Butterflies sit on the path where you walk. 3.) Don't pick the flowers. The butterflies need the nectar from flowers to survive. And 4.) Be sure to check for hitchhikers before you leave. Butterflies can land on you and catch a ride outside!

Ella took a photo of my five favorites so you could see them, too. Did you know that the monarch butterflies fly right through Iowa every fall on their long journey to Mexico? They travel more than 2,000 miles!! Along the way, monarchs can eat the nectar from just about any flower. They suck up their liquid diet with a built-in straw called a proboscis. I sure wouldn't want to drink all my meals through my nose, would you?

Yuck!
Aiden

On the fifth day of Christmas,
my cousin gave to me . . .

5 butterflies

4 big balloons, 3 train cars, 2 hefty hogs,
and a goldfinch in an oak tree.

Hi, Mom and Dad,

Did you know that the oldest covered bridge in Madison County—the Imes Bridge, built in 1870—is right in St. Charles, Ella's town? I asked Uncle Ross why the old bridges were covered, and he said it was to protect the roadway. It was cheaper to replace the roof and walls than the big heavy floor beams. Smart! Modern farm machines are too big to go through them now, so the covered bridges aren't used much anymore.

Aunt Sue took us to check out the other five bridges in Madison County. The last one we saw was the Roseman Covered Bridge. That's the one that became super famous after the book and movie The Bridges of Madison County came out. It's also the coolest bridge of them all because . . . it's haunted! In 1892, a bad guy escaped from prison and just as the sheriff's posse had him surrounded on the bridge, he rose straight up through the roof and disappeared into thin air, howling a wild cry. He was never found, and to this day he haunts the Roseman Bridge! Yikes!

Sweet dreams,
Aiden

P.S. In Iowa, everyone waves at you when they drive by, whether they know you or not. It's really nice, but my arm got a little tired today from all that waving.

On the sixth day of Christmas,
my cousin gave to me . . .

6 covered bridges

IMES BRIDGE

Cedar Bridge

Cutler-Donahoe Bridge

Holliwell Bridge

Roseman Bridge

Hogman Bridge

5 butterflies, 4 big balloons, 3 train cars, 2 hefty hogs,
and a goldfinch in an oak tree.

Dear Mom and Dad,

We loaded up our saucers and took off for a long drive to Burlington, a town on the Mississippi River. It has this crazy cobblestone road built by three Germans in 1894 that zigzags seven times down a steep hill. They call it Snake Alley, the most crooked street in the world! There is a legend that the firemen used the alley to test horses. If a horse could take all the curves at a gallop and still be breathing when it reached the top, it was allowed to haul the city's fire wagons.

Today the road was covered in snow and closed to traffic, so Ella and I joined in with other kids and had a blast sliding down! It was REALLY fun going down, but not so much fun dragging our saucers all the way back up to the top.

After sledding all afternoon, we climbed back in our car, cranked the heat way up and drove north along the great Mississippi River, which divides Iowa and Illinois. There were ice fishermen sitting on buckets and trailing their fishing lines into little holes in the ice. I was glad I was sitting in the warm car and not outside on a bucket! I sure hope they caught something!

Thanks for buying me those long johns, Mom,

Aiden

On the seventh day of Christmas,
my cousin gave to me . . .

7 saucers sliding

6 covered bridges, 5 butterflies,
4 big balloons, 3 train cars, 2 hefty hogs,
and a goldfinch in an oak tree.

Dear Mom and Dad,

Today we continued north along the Mississippi River, ending up in the far northeast corner of the state at a place called the Effigy Mounds, a prehistoric Indian burial ground near Marquette. Ancient Indian tribes patted mounds of earth into the shape of animals more than 1,000 years ago—these mounds are called effigies. More than 200 of them are preserved and 31 are shaped like bears and birds to honor loved ones and their sacred beliefs. At first it was hard to tell which animals the shapes were supposed to be because they were so BIG, but we soon made a game of it and I guessed the most right!

After our hike, we drove to Decorah to see the Vesterheim Norwegian-American Museum, which celebrates the history of people from Norway who settled in Iowa. Mom, you would have loved seeing all the painted furniture and pottery! We visited an old blacksmith shop, two log cabins, and a stone mill, but what I liked the most was learning about Julenissen (that's the name for Santa in Scandinavian countries) and his pet goat, Yuley! If you've been good all year, Yuley knocks three times on your door with his horns and Julenissen greets you with a gift. In exchange, you should have porridge ready for them before they go on to the next house. The Norwegians in the old days also believed in <u>nisses</u> (pronounced NISS-uh), mischievous elves who liked to play funny tricks on people. Ella said we probably wouldn't get to see any, but she was wrong. We saw EIGHT of them in the woods. We tiptoed away very quietly—we didn't want them to play any tricks on <u>us</u>!

Aiden

On the eighth day of Christmas, my cousin gave to me . . .

8 tricky nisses

7 saucers sliding, 6 covered bridges, 5 butterflies,
4 big balloons, 3 train cars, 2 hefty hogs,
and a goldfinch in an oak tree.

Dear Mom and Dad,

Did you know there are even farms for <u>wind</u>? We toured a wind farm in Alta today. 257 huge wind turbines towered above us— 26 stories tall, with blades the size of a jumbo jet's wings! This is one of the largest wind farms in the world, and these enormous wind machines generate as much energy as 301,000 tons of coal. Winds along Buffalo Ridge are almost constant, making it possible to supply electricity to 71,000 households in one year. Each tower produces enough energy for nearly 750 people. WOW! That's a LOT of wind.

I noticed that Uncle Ross was rummaging around in the trunk of the car and I heard him say, "Hey, this wind is good for something else, too!" He pulled out a whole bunch of brightly colored kites—enough for each of us and some other visitors, too. These weren't your average kites, though: There were dragons and snakes and alligators! As we watched our creatures dance and dart in the windy skies, Aunt Sue told us all about the "Color the Wind" winter kite festival held in Clear Lake in February. Thousands of people come from all over to fly their kites out over the frozen lake. There is even a kite show set to music! I bet it's really something to see!

Today I colored the wind,
Aiden

Dear Mom and Dad,

Today Ella took me to an indoor track where a whole bunch of cyclists were training for the longest, largest, and oldest bicycle ride in Iowa: RAGBRAI (that stands for Register's Annual Great Bicycle Ride Across Iowa). Since 1973, bicyclists of all ages ride across the state of Iowa through little towns. We joined in and did some bike training around the track with riders who were testing out the silly outfits they planned to wear for the actual ride. Some wore bumpy pickle hats or pointy witch hats stretched over their helmets, and one girl even had feathery pink wings that fluttered behind her as she rode. There were people riding unicycles, mountain bikes, speed bikes, tandem bikes, and recliner bikes.

When we took a water break, some of the riders had stories to tell of blisters and twisted ankles, but also of amazing concerts, great food, camping under the stars, and the thousands of friendly people who greeted them along their route last July. They were very excited for the next ride coming up this summer. I think it sounds like a lot of work, riding 80 miles a day, but Ella pointed out that it's a great way for families to train and exercise together and experience Iowa hospitality firsthand!

Love,
Aiden

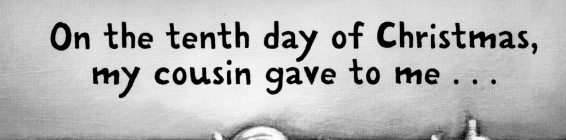

On the tenth day of Christmas, my cousin gave to me . . .

10 speedy cyclists

9 kites a-flying,
8 tricky nisses, 7 saucers sliding,
6 covered bridges, 5 butterflies, 4 big balloons,
3 train cars, 2 hefty hogs,
and a goldfinch in an oak tree.

Dear Mom and Dad,

Last night we stayed in Sioux City. From our motel, we could see a tall, pointy structure that looked just like the Washington Monument in Washington, D.C. Uncle Ross told us the monument is for Sergeant Charles Floyd, the only person who died during the Lewis and Clark Expedition (experts think he had appendicitis). We learned a lot more about his adventures at the Lewis and Clark Interactive Center. Did you know that the explorers traveled with a great big dog named Seaman who looked a lot like our dog, Harry? As we explored a day in the life of the expedition, we got our very own personal journals to record our discoveries just like Lewis and Clark did as they traveled from 1804 to 1806.

Ready to continue our own Iowa adventure, we headed up to Le Mars, the Ice Cream Capital of the World! We visited a nearby dairy where we saw 11 Holstein cows hooked up to wacky-looking machines that mechanically milked them. Then at Wells' Dairy we got to see how ice cream is made from that milk (lots of stirring!). The very best part of the day was visiting the ice cream parlor, but it was also the hardest part of the day—how to decide between so many hand-dipped flavors?? I had the biggest and best ice cream sundae EVER, with three scoops of ice cream, hot chocolate, caramel syrup, plenty of whipped cream, nuts, and a cherry on top! Yum!

Love,
Aiden, who won't need to eat for a week

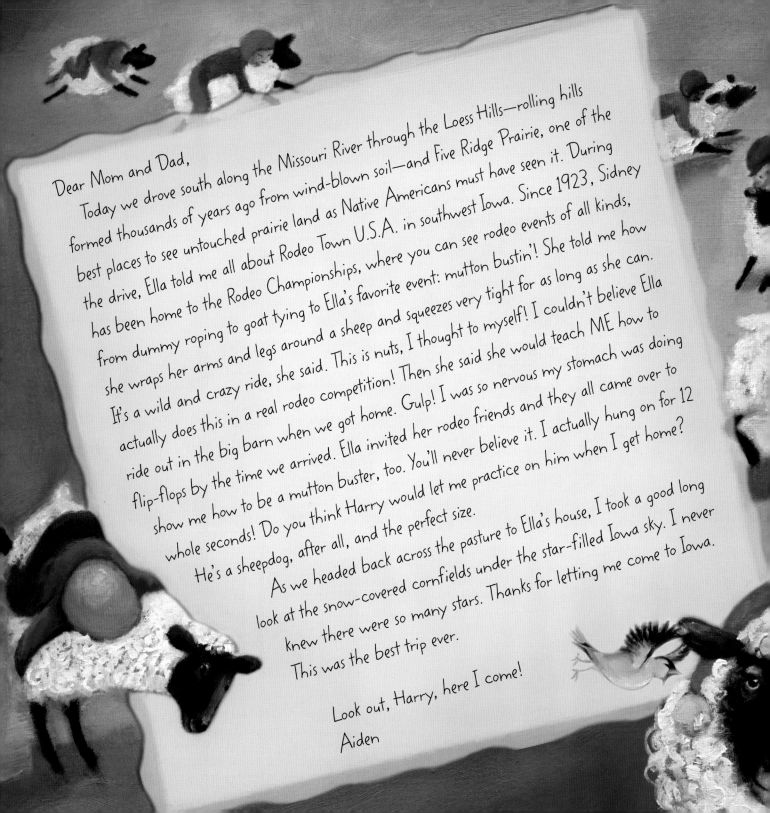

Dear Mom and Dad,

Today we drove south along the Missouri River through the Loess Hills—rolling hills formed thousands of years ago from wind-blown soil—and Five Ridge Prairie, one of the best places to see untouched prairie land as Native Americans must have seen it. During the drive, Ella told me all about Rodeo Town U.S.A. in southwest Iowa. Since 1923, Sidney has been home to the Rodeo Championships, where you can see rodeo events of all kinds, from dummy roping to goat tying to Ella's favorite event: mutton bustin'! She told me how she wraps her arms and legs around a sheep and squeezes very tight for as long as she can. It's a wild and crazy ride, she said. This is nuts, I thought to myself! I couldn't believe Ella actually does this in a real rodeo competition! Then she said she would teach ME how to ride out in the big barn when we got home. Gulp! I was so nervous my stomach was doing flip-flops by the time we arrived. Ella invited her rodeo friends and they all came over to show me how to be a mutton buster, too. You'll never believe it. I actually hung on for 12 whole seconds! Do you think Harry would let me practice on him when I get home? He's a sheepdog, after all, and the perfect size.

As we headed back across the pasture to Ella's house, I took a good long look at the snow-covered cornfields under the star-filled Iowa sky. I never knew there were so many stars. Thanks for letting me come to Iowa. This was the best trip ever.

Look out, Harry, here I come!

Aiden

On the twelfth day of Christmas,
my cousin gave to me . . .

12 mutton busters

11 cows a-milking,
10 speedy cyclists, 9 kites a-flying,
8 tricky nisses, 7 saucers sliding, 6 covered bridges,
5 butterflies, 4 big balloons, 3 train cars,
2 hefty hogs, and a goldfinch in an oak tree.

The
Hawkeye
State !

Black Hawk
1767-1838

Nordic Festival
Celebrating Decorah's
Scandinavian Heritage

CORN
STATE
Leader in
Biofuels

3 National
SPRINT C
Hall of Fam
& Museum
KNOXVIL

OUR
LIBERTIES
WE PRIZE
AND OUR
RIGHTS
WE WILL
MAINTAIN

IOWA

NORMAN BORLAUG
1914-2009

World
FOOD
Prize

Iowa State

Oldest land grant college in the USA

COME BACK AND S

IOWA
(state and river)
named after
Ioway Indians

"Is this
Heaven?"

field of
DREAMS

Elk Horn
The only working Danish
windmill in America

AMANA COLO
National Historic

ESTHERVILLE METEORITE fell to Earth in 1879 455 pounds!
TV ENTERTAINER
Johnny Carson 1925-2005
East Peru
First Red Delicious
GRANT WOOD
1891-1942
AMERICAN PAINTER best known for "American Gothic"
BILY AMAZING BROTHERS CLOCKS SPILLVILLE, IA.
Strawberry Point
World's Largest Strawberry
Glenn Miller Famous Jazz Musician Band leader • Trombonist
1904-1944
US SOON!
First Lady
Mamie Doud Eisenhower 1896-1979
oak
GEODE
Laura Ingalls Wilder Park • Museum • Burr Oak
Le Mars
ICE CREAM CAPITAL of the WORLD

Iowa: The Hawkeye State

Capital and largest city: Des Moines • **State abbreviation:** IA • **State bird:** the Eastern goldfinch • **State tree:** the oak • **State rock:** the geode • **State song:** "Song of Iowa" • **State flower:** the wild prairie rose • **State motto:** "Our liberties we prize, and our rights we will maintain"

Some Famous Iowans:

Leon "Bix" Beiderbecke (1903–1931), born in Davenport, always loved music. As a teenager, he often sat on the banks of the Mississippi River to listen to the riverboat bands. Bix got his big break recording with the Wolverine Orchestra in 1924, eventually becoming a well-known jazz cornetist, pianist, and composer.

Amelia Bloomer (1818–1894) gave voice to the growing movement of people demanding equal rights for women. Her name was made even more famous when she created a loose, comfortable women's undergarment—known as "bloomers"—to replace the cumbersome petticoats that women were expected to wear at the time. Amelia and her family moved to Iowa in 1855, and she died in Council Bluffs.

George Washington Carver (c. 1864–1943) was a scientist, botanist, educator, and inventor, whose studies revolutionized agriculture in the South. He studied botany at Iowa Agricultural College (now Iowa State University), and became the school's first African-American faculty member. He is best known for his research into the use of peanuts. Some even say he was the inventor of peanut butter!

"Buffalo Bill" Cody (1846–1917), born in LeClaire, was a famous frontiersman and traveling showman. His hugely popular "Wild West" shows were designed to both educate and entertain using a cast of hundreds, including real Native American chiefs, cowboys, and cowgirls, as well as live buffalo, elk, and cattle.

Dan Gable (1948–) is a popular amateur wrestler best known for winning a gold medal at the 1972 Olympics. As a coach, he won 15 NCAA team titles and 21 straight Big Ten titles at the University of Iowa. The Dan Gable International Wrestling Institute and Museum is in Waterloo, where Dan was born.

Shawn Johnson (1992–), born in Des Moines, is the 2008 Olympic balance beam gold medalist and individual all-around silver medalist, 2007 all-around World Champion, and 2007/08 U.S. all-around champion. She trains at Chow's Gymnastics and Dance Institute in West Des Moines.

John Wayne (1907–1979), whose given name was Marion Morrison, was born in Winterset. The son of a pharmacist, he grew up to be an Academy Award®- and Golden Globe Award®-winning actor in Hollywood. His rugged masculine roles made him an enduring American icon.

To my husband, Ross (my favorite Iowan), our children,
and to the friendly folks who make up this great state of Iowa.
—S.C.

Acknowledgments:
A big thank you to Mary Conklin at the National Balloon Museum in Indianola
for her help verifying information about balloon competitions,
to Natalie Cooley for information about mutton busting
and raising baby pigs for the Iowa State Fair,
and to my powerhouse editorial/design quintet: Meredith Mundy, Andrea Santoro,
Kate Moll, Katrina Damkoehler, and NaNá Stoeltze.

STERLING and the distinctive Sterling logo are registered trademarks of Sterling Publishing Co., Inc.

Library of Congress Cataloging-in-Publication Data
Cornelison, Sue.
The twelve days of Christmas in Iowa / written and illustrated by Susan F. Cornelison.   p. cm.
Summary: Aiden writes a letter home each of the twelve days he spends exploring Iowa at Christmastime, as his cousin Ella
shows him everything from a goldfinch in an oak tree to twelve "mutton busters." Includes facts about Iowa.
ISBN 978-1-4027-6710-4
1. Iowa—Juvenile fiction. [1. Iowa—Fiction. 2. Christmas—Fiction. 3. Cousins—Fiction. 4. Letters—Fiction.] I. Title.
PZ7.C816344Twe 2010   [E] —dc22
2009012129

Lot#:
2 4 6 8 10 9 7 5 3 1
06/10
Published by Sterling Publishing Co., Inc. 387 Park Avenue South, New York, NY 10016
Text and illustrations © 2010 by Sue F. Cornelison
The original illustrations for this book were created using oil paints.
Distributed in Canada by Sterling Publishing
c/o Canadian Manda Group, 165 Dufferin Street, Toronto, Ontario, Canada M6K 3H6
Distributed in the United Kingdom by GMC Distribution Services
Castle Place, 166 High Street, Lewes, East Sussex, England BN7 1XU
Distributed in Australia by Capricorn Link (Australia) Pty. Ltd. P.O. Box 704, Windsor, NSW 2756, Australia

Printed in China

Sterling ISBN 978-1-4027-6710-4

For information about custom editions, special sales, premium and corporate purchases, please contact
Sterling Special Sales Department at 800-805-5489 or specialsales@sterlingpublishing.com.

Designed by Kate Moll.

CANADA

Washington

Montana

Oregon

Idaho

Wyoming

Nevada

Utah

Colorado

California

Arizona

New Mexico

Alaska

Hawaii

MEXICO

(NOT TO SCALE)